LOADED LACES

AN EAGLES HOCKEY NOVELLA

ELISE FABER

EAGLES HOCKEY SERIES

Eagles Hockey Series (all stand alone)
Broken Laces
Lace 'em Up
Knotted Laces
Loaded Laces
Lucky Laces

ONE

West

I CAN'T BELIEVE she's here, asking *that*.

The locker room is packed, full of reporters and bloggers, all of whom are looking for their next viral moment, and Isabelle—Belle—Harrison is here with her phone shoved close to my face, the screen showing she's recording our conversation, all while she's asking *that*.

I grind my teeth, striving for patience.

For control.

Because I haven't seen this woman since we were both sixteen and she dumped me right before I got on the bus for my first game in the juniors.

I spent the long ass drive through frozen plains, desperate for a mountain or lake or rolling hill and only seeing dry and white and snow-covered, all while nursing a broken heart.

No. Not broken.

Eviscerated. Shredded. Stomped on.

Then...the anger came.

By the time I hit the ice, I was pissed. An angry mother-fucker who wanted to draw blood—probably why I went out and had my best game ever.

And I haven't seen her since.

Until now.

Until she's asking a question I don't want to fucking answer.

The only positive to this shit show is that no one is paying attention to us.

The one reporter who was hovering near her shoulder, closing in, trying to edge her out has given up and moved on to another player, and because I'm not one of the stars on the team, Belle and the male reporter were the only two interested in speaking to me after the game.

Meanwhile, Rome is surrounded, everyone wanting a sound bite from our captain.

King is similarly encircled, his last name, Bang, synonymous with hockey royalty. He and his four brothers all play in the league, and their father before them had made his name in the NHL first.

The Bang Brothers are famous...and *infamous*.

And King is going to surpass all of them in records and games played and points garnered.

Me? I'm a grinder.

I'm living the dream—I'm doing the job I fantasized about as a little kid. I have a house, a nice car, money in the bank, and I'm secure in my life.

So, of course she's here *now*.

Asking that shit.

I glance to the right, see that my teammates are occupied with each other and the rest of the press corps.

Then I glance to the left, seeing a similar scene playing out.

Then I make a split second decision.

I stand up.

Okay, so that may not seem like much of a decision, but standing isn't the only thing I do—or *plan* to do, anyway.

Of course, Belle derails that.

Funny that.

Her derailing my plans.

It's like she's born to do it.

Like she's *planned* to.

When I stand, I do it quickly, so quickly that she stumbles backward, eyes going wide.

Mine aren't wide. They're dragging down the front of her body—noticing that while her face has barely aged over the last decade, her body sure as fuck has grown up.

She's curved in all the right places. Tits I want to bury my face in. Hips that are perfectly shaped so that I can hold on tight as I plunge deep. God, I bet her ass is fantastic.

I don't get the chance to appreciate it, though.

Because she's still skittering backward...toward the Eagles logo on the carpet.

"Fuck," I mutter.

I sway forward, wrapping an arm around her middle, drawing her to a halt.

"Wh—?"

"Don't step on the logo," I mutter.

"The what—?" She freezes, eyes going wide again, head jerking to look over her shoulder and down at the eagle emblazoned on the floor. "Oh," she whispers. "The *logo.*"

I nod, and I know I have a choice—I can release her, ignore her question, finish getting changed, and go home to my nice house, my nice life, my nice bank account. *Or* I can do...

What I do next.

Which is to say, I don't *really* have a choice.

I've already made the decision.

I tighten my arm around her middle, draw her flush against me, enjoying the feel of those lush tits against my side for a moment before she starts protesting and I start moving, bringing her along with me as I slip out of the locker room door and into the hall.

The space is quiet, all the action taking place inside where the guys and press are.

Still, I know it's a lucky coincidence.

After games are busy times, and it's only a matter of time before someone comes along.

Which is why I move quickly, dragging her forward, ignoring her sputtered protests, and shoving through one of the doors.

I release her once we're inside the empty office, flicking on the lights as I close the door behind us.

Then I turn to the woman who broke my heart and ask a question of my own,

"What the fuck are you doing here after all this time, Belle?"

TWO

Belle

RIGHT.

So, I may have underestimated the all-grown-up-now West Stevenson.

May have underestimated the boy who'd been my first love and how much he'd changed.

Once he'd been devoted to me, would have grown wings and flown to the moon and back, picked his way through the Sahara in soul-crushing sandstorms, crawled for miles over broken glass…he would have done all those cliché idioms about love and devotion for me without a second thought.

Which was why I had to let him go.

But that's not why I'm here today.

This whole thing is dumb, probably the stupidest thing I've ever done.

But…I'm desperate.

And—

I stifle my sigh.

I'm *desperate*. I have no other choice and I'm fucking desperate and I had to know that he was still the same West as a decade ago.

"*Belle*," he growls, and I jump.

"I—" But I don't go any further. Because I can't summon any words, an explanation that makes this make sense—me being here, me starting shit.

Because it *doesn't* make sense.

Except to say that I'm the aforementioned *desperate*.

"Why the fuck are you here?" he snaps. "Or should I say, why the fuck are you here asking that insulting ass question?"

Desperate.

D.E.S.P.E.R.A.T.E.

"*Belle!*" he growls again and I jump again. But this time it unsticks the words in my head.

"I wanted to..."

Just as easily as the words came, the rest of my sentence fades out.

Probably because it ends with *ask you a favor*.

Fuck.

My chest goes tight, and I struggle to hold his gaze, guilt rippling through me. I can't screw up his life like this. Not when I already hurt him so badly all those years ago.

His hands settle onto the outsides of my arms, gripping me firmly. Not painfully.

But firmly.

And as though he wants to shake me until I finish what I was going to say.

"I'm just a bitch," I say, and it's not exactly a lie. The last decade hasn't made me sweet, hasn't made me pliable and easy-going. It's made me a fighter.

And increasingly isolated.

His brows flick up in surprise, or maybe in question, but I don't miss it in his eyes—the concern.

For me.

Crap.

That seals it.

"I wanted to push your buttons, knew I had the ammunition to do it." I shrug, know it's sure to piss him off, to distract him from all the things I don't want him to see. "I was hoping for my viral moment. Gotta get those sponsors, you know."

Something slithers through his gray eyes.

But it's something I don't recognize, and not because it's here and gone in an instant.

Mostly it's because suddenly he's encroaching on my space, his big frame bending, his face in mine, a thunderstorm in his eyes.

"Liar," he whispers.

Right.

I already knew this was dumb.

Now I know I need to end this.

"Since I didn't get that viral moment," I say, lifting my chin and deliberately taking a step back, breaking his hold on me, "I'll go."

Silence, charged and hot and taut, fills the room.

"You'll go." Quiet words.

"Yes."

"You'll *go.*"

Quiet words that are laced with such rage that I take another step back.

"Oh, no," he mutters, reaching out and snagging my wrist. "You're not just *going.*"

I open my mouth, jerk at his grip, but it's useless.

A moment later, he's spinning us and all the air whooshes out of my lungs as I find myself pressed to the closed door, his body flush against mine. "You don't get to do this, to show up out of the fucking blue, asking that shit, and then waltzing right the fuck back out again."

What's wrong with me that his furious words slide like velvet over my skin?

That I wonder how else he might have changed, might have *grown?*

If his hold shifted, if his hands skated down my body, slid into my clothes, and he fucked me right against this door, I know I wouldn't protest.

I know I would enjoy it.

Crave it.

Love it.

That was the problem before.

"Now, you've always been a shit liar, Belle—"

My eyes close, both at the knowledge that hasn't always been true and because the nickname...

God, I've missed it.

He's the only person to ever call me that—the only person I allowed to have that.

Hearing it now...

No.

I can't have it, can't *allow* myself to have it.

I force my lids back open, force myself to hold his gaze as he continues talking.

"—so just cut the crap and give in." He bends closer, his hair tumbling over his forehead, his gray eyes blazing. "Tell me why you're here, baby."

That desperation creeps back in, but I attempt to beat it back.

"Tell. Me," he growls.

My attempts at escaping continue to fail, panic crawls through my insides, a lie coming to the tip of my tongue. "I—"

"No lies," he snaps, cutting me off. "No bullshit. Just fucking *tell* me."

And the desperation takes control.

THREE

ONE SECOND, I'm pinning her to the door.

The next, I'm curled in a ball, gripping...well, my *balls*.

Christ, even with a cup she still managed to get both of them.

Groaning, I roll over to my hands and knees, struggling to sit up, but I manage it just as the door shuts with a soft *click*.

"Fuck," I mutter, groaning again as I lurch up to my feet and reach for the handle.

I'm twisting it and taking off after her in the next instant, my gait uneven for a few paces before I manage to shake off the pain and head toward the exit, thankful that I took my skates off earlier, that I don't have to worry about dulling the blades by walking on something that isn't the black mats that lead from the locker rooms down to the ice.

But, truthfully, I wouldn't give a fuck what kind floor I'm walking on as I haul ass after Belle.

I'd take whatever verbal reaming the equipment guys

would lay on me for ruining my skate blades, no matter how brutal it was.

I turn the corner just in time to see a flash of brown hair gleaming in the overhead lights, spreading out behind her like a cape as she takes a right down another hallway—this one being the one that leads out to the underground parking garage.

Which means she's close to making it to her car.

Close to escaping.

I grind my teeth together, push through the fatigue sinking into my body, my legs from an intense game against the Sierra, *and* ignore the ache in my balls, then speed up until I'm sprinting down the corridor, turning the corner—

The exit door slams shut.

"Fuck," I mutter again, but I don't stop, reaching the door a heartbeat after it latches, slamming my hands against the metal bar that opens it, shoving the panel wide, gaze searching the hushed, darkened parking lot.

There.

I whip to the left, hustle several rows over, and see Belle struggling to insert a key into the door of a piece of shit car. The sedan is so fucking rusted and taped together—literally taped together with duct tape—that it's a miracle it somehow managed to make it into the underground garage at all.

I half expect the handle to be torn free as she wrestles with that key, gets the door to unlock, and yanks it open.

But it stays in place and the heavy panel swings wide, and—

She gasps.

Because I've thrown out my hand to catch it. "I know you're in a hurry, sweet cheeks," I drawl, "but I don't think Huddy will appreciate you denting his ride."

It's a sweet ride too, a Porsche he somehow crams his big body into.

I prefer the leg room in my Land Rover.

"I need to go," she says quietly.

"You need to go." I let the words hang in the air, my unspoken question—you need to go after showing up after all these years, saying that shit?—sitting heavy between us.

I know she feels it because her throat works, eyes dancing away.

"I didn't mean to hurt you," she whispers. "And I know I shouldn't have come here."

"Then why did you?"

More silence, her unspoken answer to my question weighing the conversation down even further.

I want to shake her, want to force her to give me a fucking explanation.

But I've never been able to make Belle do anything she doesn't want to do—not ten years ago when we were teenagers —and I know I have no hope of making that happen with this stranger—yet not—standing in front of me.

So, I wait.

And I hope that I can wait her out.

Her one weakness...patience.

She burns hot, makes rash decisions—

Burned. Made.

The reminder is a visceral slap.

I don't know this woman in front of me, this woman from my past, this woman who left a wound so vast that no matter how much I tried to bury it, to ignore it, was still there, still aching, still oozing out sickness into my soul.

Because she doesn't speak.

Just keeps her pretty brown eyes on mine and *doesn't speak.*

"Let's start with something easy," I say, breaking the silence, biting back my frustration. "Do you live here?"

Those eyes slide to the side.

Then come back to mine.

"Define *here*," she replies.

Progress. And...not. I stifle a sigh. "You're really going to pull that shit now?"

"No," she says and the ice in her tone, the tart that slips across the space and jabs at me makes my dick hard. I'm a sick fuck, what can I say? But I've always loved it when this woman gives me attitude, always loved it because it meant I could kiss her until she went soft for me...

Then could kiss her some more.

"No," she says again, tart intensifying. "What I'm going to do is go home—"

"So you *do* live here in town."

She stills, eyes going wide, clearly realizing her mistake.

Not that she lets me sit in that victory.

Her chin lifts. "I'm leaving."

She turns for the open door again, yanking at the panel.

I hold it fast, but something in the back seat draws my focus.

Movement.

A jerk at the door. A hand shoving at my chest. "Let. *Go*," she grunts.

But I'm not paying attention to Belle right now.

I'm staring through the back window of that shitty fucking car, trying to discern what's making that movement...

And then I *do*.

Because I see a kid who's all of nine or ten slowly sitting up, hair disheveled, eyes sleepy—

Gray eyes sleepy.

Everything in me locks down.

And then bursts free when I hear,

"Mom?"

FOUR

Belle

I HEAR QUINN'S VOICE, and ice spreads out through my insides.

Not the fake cold I slap on to keep everyone at bay, but the real shit, the terror that grips tightly in iron claws and shakes and shakes and *shakes* until I'm torn open and my insides are spilling out onto the floor.

Dumb.

I'm so fucking dumb.

Fingers wrap around my arm. *Tightly.*

"Mom?" West growls.

"You're hurting me," I whisper, though he's not. Not really. Still, his hold immediately loosens.

"*Mom?*" I hear again, worry in Quinn's voice.

He's smart, my kid, so fucking smart that there's no way that he didn't pick up on the scene or the tension.

"Buckle up, kid," I tell him. "We're going."

"Mom—"

"*Now*, kid."

It's said in my Mom Tone, a tone I don't pull out regularly—which is lucky for me today because it means that Quinn listens without further protest, and I hear his belt click as I lean in, jam the keys in the ignition and start up the engine. "I'll just be a minute."

He opens his mouth but one look has it clicking closed again.

I straighten out of the car, close the door, then turn back to the man who's positively vibrating with rage behind me. West is beautiful in his anger, the dark slashes of his eyebrows as he glares at me, the stubble on his cheeks calling for a woman's fingers, the hard lines of his jaw, his cheekbones, his nose that whisper for gentle kisses.

"Do not fucking tell me—"

I step close, settling my hand on his chest, and tamp down on my idiocy, my shame, and give him what he needs to know.

"He's not yours."

West had been in the process of reaching down, readying to remove my hand from his body, if the tight fingers around my wrist are any indication.

My words have him freezing.

"Whose then?" he rasps.

Bile rises, burning a path in my throat.

"Not yours," I push out, knowing that even though I try to force my tone back to normal, try to make this all seem casual and no big deal (and circling back to *delusional*), I fail miserably. "That's all you need to know."

His eyes tell me he knows I'm lying.

But he doesn't call me on it.

Instead, he flicks his gaze to the rear window.

My eyes follow his, see that Quinn is watching us.

"I need to go," I tell him.

"If you honestly think that I'm letting you go after showing up in my locker room—"

"It's not yours," I mutter.

His brows flick up in question.

"It's the *Eagles'* locker room," I tell him.

A flash of irritation through his eyes. "And am I not a player for the Eagles?"

I don't know why I'm even arguing about this. "I'm going to go."

"You're not just leaving," he snaps. "Not after that scene in the locker room, not after all these years."

"You don't get to have an opinion about what I'm going to do."

"Right," he mutters.

My brows drag together—because he's agreeing with me all of a sudden? But before I get the chance to get the hell out of here, he's reaching forward, yanking open the door, and tearing my keys from the ignition.

"What are you—?"

He turns, looks in the back seat. "You as confused as I am, kid?"

"Quinn," I begin.

Neither of them look at me.

"Yeah," Quinn mutters.

"Good," West says, reaching forward and yanking at the lock for the back door. "Then let's all go inside and we'll sort this out."

Quinn unbuckles and pushes open the door, slipping out before I can stop him.

"I—"

Another beat as they both ignore me.

"Quinn—"

My kid glances back over my shoulder at me, expression telling me I'm not going to like what he says next.

And it's true.

I don't.

Because it's a lie.

"I need to use the bathroom, Mom," he says as he follows West back toward the arena.

A throb in my temple, and no, I don't know the inner working of my son's bladder, but he's nine. He's not a toddler going through potty training. We watched the game, and though he ate his body weight in snacks and drank a jug of soda, he also used the bathroom before we walked to the car and I left him out here to wait.

Mom of the year, I know.

But it's barely been an hour.

I know nature's not calling.

And...this is the only safe place I could leave him.

I have a press pass, which means I have access to park in this gated structure beneath the arena.

And I couldn't leave my kid in an open, unmanned parking lot while waiting to ask the only man I've ever loved a huge favor he has no need to grant me.

Hell, if anything, he'd be stupid as shit to help me after all I did to him.

But I had to ask.

For Quinn, I *had* to ask.

Only now, as I watch the two of them take off across the lot, move to the door to the arena, and walk inside, I know—

Like everything else in my life...

I've gone and fucked that up too.

FIVE

West

"WAIT HERE A SECOND, KID," I order quietly as I move into the dressing room—this being different than the locker room where the press congregate for interviews.

Different because it's where we all shower and change, and the last thing the kid needs to see is a bunch of naked dudes.

I watch him nod then lean back against the wall.

Good.

I move straight to my stall, rip off the rest of my gear, ignoring the curious look that Huddy tosses my way, and get dressed in record time.

"You good?" he asks as I yank up a pair of sweats, not bothering to take the time to put my suit back on.

I'll get the rest of my shit tomorrow.

Sneakers on, keys and wallet in my pockets, jacket in my hand.

"I'm good," I mutter.

I smell like shit and need a shower like I need my next breath, but I've been worse.

I move back out into the hall before anyone else can stop me and find that the kid hasn't moved.

Belle has, though.

She's standing between her son and the door.

I consider my options then start walking back down the hall.

"Are we supposed to just keep trailing you like puppies?" she asks, her tone *all* attitude. "Or are you going to give me my keys back?"

I turn the corner, shove open a door, and nod to the kid. "Bathroom."

His eyes fill with guilt, telling me that what he'd told his mom outside was a lie. But he steps inside, closes the door, and I back up, leaning against the opposite wall.

A hand appears in front of my face.

"Keys," Belle demands.

The toilet flushes, and I hear the sink go. Good kid. Trained well.

"You going to tell me why he has my eyes if he's not mine?"

Her eyes deliberately avoid mine.

Same as I *deliberately* keep her keys in my pocket.

The door opens, and I glance down at the kid. "Good?"

He nods.

Belle sighs.

I start walking.

Only, when I push out the door, I don't lead us back to Belle's piece-of-shit car. I head straight for my SUV.

"What are you doing, West?" she snaps.

"You came all this way, after all these years pulling this shi —" She stiffens and flicks her gaze to the side. To the kid.

"*Stuff*," I correct. "And it was important enough to come here now, after"—I flick my brows up—"*everything* that went down between us..."

She sucks in a breath.

"Since you did all that"—I hold her eyes—"we're going to talk about it. And we can't do it in a parking lot."

"I—"

"It's late. I'm beat. Your kid needs to get horizontal. He can do that in the spare room at my place, or he can do it at your place, but I'll drive you both there then take off when it's sorted."

"What about my car?"

She makes a good point.

It would make sense for her to drive her car where we're going to talk. But we need to actually *talk*. Which means I can't let her drive on her own, otherwise she's likely to disappear again and the next time she *re*appears, it'll be with something worse than a question and a kid who supposedly isn't mine but who has my eyes.

"I'll have someone get it back to wherever you end up tonight."

Even if that's me taking an Uber back here and driving the POS to her place.

Then, before she can argue any further, I hit the locks for my car, open the back door for the kid. Quinn, to his credit, glances at his mom.

Christ, she's beautiful.

And furious.

But she tables the anger and jerks her head toward the open door.

Only then does Quinn hop into the back seat, and I see him reach for the belt, buckle up.

Good kid.

I shut the door, glance back at her and lift my eyebrows.

She sighs then stomps around the back of my SUV and climbs into the front seat, slamming the door hard enough that the entire vehicle rocks. My lips twitch.

When she used to have attitude like this, I'd draw her close and kiss her until she stopped being mad. I wasn't all that good at it back then, the kissing, the sex, but I learned how to take care of her, learned what she liked, learned how to hold off getting my pleasure before she got hers.

I reckon I can kiss a lot better nowadays.

And that I'd be a lot better at giving her pleasure before losing hold on mine.

Shoving that thought down, I yank open my door, climb inside.

"Your place or mine?"

There's a sudden burst of tension, coming from both the front seat and back, but Belle's voice is quiet when she says, "Yours."

I wait a beat, wonder if either of them will say anything else.

When they don't, I turn on the ignition and pull out of the garage, driving out of the downtown area and up into the rolling green hills. She's staring out the window, and not a word is spoken by either of them as I go—though, I think for Quinn's sake, that's mostly because his nose is buried in his phone, the flashes of light from the back seat telling me that he's playing a game. In Belle's silence, I can't read anything aside from pissed, but I don't miss that as each mile passes, the tension in her body ratchets up until she's a fucking statue in the passenger's seat.

Pissed and...something else I haven't teased out yet.

I hit the clicker to open the garage, pull inside, and shut off the ignition.

Then I'm leading them into my house.

"There's an Xbox in the family room," I say, pointing across the hall. "If you and your mom are both cool with it, you can play while your mom and I talk." I walk to the pantry, push open the door, and flick on the lights. "Help yourself to any food in here or"—I nod at the fridge—"there. Drinks are in the door or the fridge in the island."

Quinn's eyes are wide then he turns to his mom and I know he's seeing the same thing I am—a woman who looks freaked the fuck out. "Maybe I should stay while you two are talking," he whispers.

Good kid. Smart kid.

"Up to your mom," I say going to the fridge and grabbing out two chocolate milks and a Diet Coke. I offer him one before I set the Diet Coke in front of Belle on the counter.

"*You* drink chocolate milk?" he asks, mouth dropping open.

"Best post-game snack on the planet," I say, shoving the straw in and drinking deeply. "Nice that it doesn't taste bad either."

He grins, starts in on his own milk.

Pop!

I turn, see that Belle has tabled her freakout and is drinking from the can. With a quiet "Ah!" she sets it on the counter then she nods at Quinn. "No first person shooters," she says softly, and it takes me a moment to realize she's talking about the type of game he's allowed to play. "But free rein on the rest of the Xbox."

"Really?" he asks, eyes lighting up.

Her mouth hitches up. "Really." He starts to turn for the other room, pauses when she adds, "So long as you promise that you'll put it down when you get tired and sprawl out on the couch."

I don't comment as he nods.

I also don't comment on the fact that her words indicate this conversation is going to take a while.

I just drink my chocolate milk.

And I wait.

SIX

Belle

I HEAR the video game turn on and suck back my soda for
courage.

He remembered I'm addicted to it.

Will drink it any time of day—or *had* drank it any time of
day before shit got real and my budget meant that I couldn't
afford it.

Now, it's an indulgence that's few and far between.

Food for my kid, drinks for my kid and *then* stuff for me.

It's how it should be.

It's not how *I* had it, but it's how West had it—good parents,
people who looked out for him, who loved him, who loved *me*...

At least until I drove them all away.

But I still kept him, kept them...in Quinn—giving him the
love he needed, giving him everything I could.

And that all worked great.

Until Quinn got sick.

And the bills piled up.

And I was evicted.

And I was—*am*—desperate.

"I shouldn't have gone to the rink," I begin, setting my can onto the counter with a soft *click*.

"Why's that?"

So many reasons.

So many that I can't immediately answer.

He sighs when the silence stretches and comes close, resting a hip against the cabinets. He's all of three feet away from me but he may as well be on the other side of the Grand Canyon.

And I did that. *I created that gulf between us.*

But he doesn't push—just keeps leaning against the counter, keeps looking at me.

Keeps *waiting*.

It's stifling, that attention. Painful, the memories. Terrifying, being here.

And yet...I have nowhere else to go.

And those are the words that slide off my tongue, drift through the air.

"I have nowhere else to go," I whisper, tracing my finger through the condensation on the side of the can, creating nonsensical patterns on the aluminum. "*We* have nowhere else to go."

He had been leaning, his arms and ankles lazily crossed, but my words have him straightening. "What do you mean that you have nowhere else to go?" His voice is quiet, his eyes flicking toward the family room.

"Quinn—"

My voice cracks, tears filling my eyes. "He knows," I whisper. "I tried to hide it from him, spin it as an adventure. But..." I exhale, try to blink back the tears.

"He's smart."

I nod, a bolt of warmth sliding through me at the matter-of-factness in West's tone. "He's smart," I agree. "He figured it out, even though I tried to shield him from the reality of our situation."

"And what *is* the reality of your situation, Belle?"

A quiet question, but one that's as insidious as what I'd asked him earlier in the locker room.

I force my eyes to remain on his as I say, "The reality is that I have nothing but the car back at the arena and our bags of clothes in the trunk. And Quinn," I whisper. "I have Quinn, who's everything."

West's expression is unreadable. "Where's Quinn's dad?"

I sigh. Because it's a fair question. Because I wish I knew.

"He was a one-night stand," I say softly.

The silence that falls between us is terrible. "Right after you left—" He jerks and I hurry to go on, "I couldn't hack it at home any longer. My parents were..." I shake my head. "They were themselves, and your parents were upset for you, obviously."

He jerks again.

"So, I finished my junior year, waited it out until I turned eighteen that summer. Then I used my savings to buy a car, packed up my stuff, and got the hell out of there. I didn't tell anyone I was leaving, didn't bother with my senior year, and I certainly didn't graduate"—something that's come back to bite me time and again during my job searches over the last decade —"I just...left. And for a while, it was great. I had all the confidence of a newly turned eighteen-year-old with no fear and a joy for everything that I was experiencing—the open road, lots of odd jobs, sleeping under the stars, seeing all the things I dreamed of."

"Yellowstone?" he asks softly.

My heart spasms—he remembered that too—but I nod,

force myself to keep going. "Yes," I murmur. "I spent six months in Wyoming, working and saving up money so I could keep moving west, and I did it spending every single free moment seeing all that Yellowstone has to offer."

"Was it what you wanted it to be?"

"Better." My mind drifts, bringing me back to that time. "It's so vast and varied and, aside from holding Quinn that first time, I've never experienced something so awe-inspiring and beautiful. Not before or since."

"I'm glad you had that."

I shake myself, realize that West has come closer—near enough that he brushes away a rogue tear that has escaped and is skating down my cheek.

"It's where I met Quinn's dad," I tell him. "I was working at a restaurant in Jackson, picking up a couple of shifts before I moved on and...I did something rash. He flirted. I flirted back and"—a breath to shore myself up—"I took him back to the room I was renting. But the condom broke and"—I force myself to keep my eyes open, to hold this man's gaze—"he left while I was cleaning up and I never saw him again. Stupid, huh?"

West's face is gentle. "You were a kid—stupid kind of goes along with that."

I smile begrudgingly. "You're not wrong."

His soft laughter is one of the best sounds I've ever head.

I always loved making him laugh.

That unsticks something in me, and the words I never wanted to say aloud slip out, "He looked like you."

West's mouth drops open.

"He had your eyes and he was strong and...I let myself pretend that night."

"Baby."

"But he wasn't you," I whisper. "Though he gave me the best gift of my life."

"Baby."

"I waited for him to show up," I go on, having to finish this. "But when he didn't come back after a few months...I knew I had to move on. My car wasn't equipped for winter somewhere that actually snows, and the drive to my doctor alone would be dangerous once the weather turned. So, I headed for sunnier climates and better social services and schools and...somewhere I would just be another face, rather than the girl who got pregnant."

And I made it work. It was hard, but eventually, I found work as an assistant. It was—*is*—demanding. But it's also fun and challenging and I like my boss.

"We were steady. Stable. Always riding that razor's edge but surviving. I even put money away for Quinn for college"— money, that if I was able to touch again because it wasn't in his protected account would have saved us from the eviction—"but then Quinn got sick and I had to take paid family leave and FMLA." He jerks. "He's okay now," I hurry to add. "He had a really bad infection and spent nearly two months in the hospital, but he's okay."

"I'm glad, baby."

I nod. "So while my job was safe, I only got seventy percent of that pay during that time and..." I bite the inside of my cheek. "That razor's edge...it cut." More tears slip free.

He touches my cheek again, catching them as they fall. "You don't have to tell me the rest."

Except...I do.

Because I need him to understand.

"And then my car bit it. That was the death knell. I had to buy the beater you saw that barely runs because it was all I could afford. And buying it meant I got further behind on everything—rent, work, those medical bills." Shame ripples over me. "I tried everything—food pantries, negotiating with the hospital to lower the debt, making installment payments. I applied for grants, begged my landlord..."

His hand finds mine.

"Today was the day we had to leave our apartment," I say softly. "And Quinn won tickets to the game tonight, and I knew we couldn't go home, same as I knew that I had no business taking him to the game. But he *won* the tickets at a raffle at school and, yes, my boy has a phone and he has food in his belly, but he's never had *that*—never gone to a sports game, never sat in great seats, never had souvenir snacks or a hat with a hockey team emblazoned on the front..."

It's all secondhand clothes and store-brand foods and far too many cans of beans.

"And then," I whisper, "I saw you out there on the ice."

SEVEN

West

"...I saw you out there on the ice."

My heart skips a beat.

"I hadn't realized you'd been traded to the Eagles—"

"Right before the season started," I murmur.

She nods, takes a breath, and goes on, "And I thought, *God* —" She shoves a hand through her hair, and I wince at how tightly she grips the strands. "I was so fucking stupid. I have a press pass because I assisted my boss at an event last week, and I thought you..."

I wait, lungs tight.

A shake of her head. "I was desperate and I went to you and I fucked it up because I knew that I couldn't ask you for help, not after what I did, after how I ended things."

Another tear escapes and I can't stand here like this any longer.

Separate.

Watching her hurt.

Not holding her.

"We were kids, baby," I say, moving closer, tucking my arm around her shoulders and drawing her against me. "We were young and in love and who knows if we would have gone the distance?"

Her words are barely audible. "You wanted to make that happen."

"I did," I agree, smoothing my hand up and down her back. "And, yeah, it took me a few years to understand the whys of our breakup, but I got there and I'm not pissed about it."

"You were pissed in the locker room."

"Because you showed up out of the blue with accusations in your eyes and barbed words on your tongue."

She exhales and it's sharp. "I know." It's a whisper before her head tilts back and she glances up at me. "I'm sorry. And I'm sorry about how I ended things."

I hate that I can feel the bumps of her spine as I stroke her back, vow to make my first order of business (*after* I get her and Quinn set up in my guest rooms) is to get more food in her on the regular. "Like I said, Belle, it took me a bit to understand what you were doing and *why* you were doing it—"

She lifts her head, pretty eyes widening.

"My mom told me what she said to you." I tuck a strand of hair behind her ear. "She still feels guilty about it, baby."

"She was right," Belle murmurs. "We were too young, and you needed to focus on building your life, not on a girlfriend back home."

"She wanted you to build your life too."

Belle inhales deeply, holding the breath in her lungs for long enough that I have to table the urge to shake her and remind her to breathe.

Then, fucking finally, she exhales.

"I did build a life, honey."

I think of medical debt and the eviction, the bumps on her spine and shadows in eyes I used to know better than my own.

She hasn't built a life to live.

She's spent all these years surviving.

And I'm going to do something about it.

I cup her cheek, tilt her head up so her eyes come back to mine. "Let's forget about the past. For tonight, anyway," I add when I see the protest well up in her expression. "I have plenty of guest rooms. You and Quinn each lay claim to one until your next move is decided, yeah?"

She's still, so still I have to resist that urge to shake again.

"I can't ask you to—"

"You didn't." A beat. "Which means you're going to take me up on my offer of hospitality and not argue. Just for tonight," I add when I see another protest creep into her face.

Her eyes close and she's quiet for a long, long moment.

Then she sighs.

And I know I've won.

"Just for tonight," she murmurs.

I SET the box of donuts on the counter and turn for the coffee pot, not surprised when I hear hurried footsteps and Belle's hushed voice.

"We need to move, baby, if we're going to catch the bus and get you to school on time."

I'm pouring myself a cup of coffee as she skids into the kitchen, eyes wide and worried, Quinn looking sleepy and rumpled as he affects a zombie, slowly trailing her.

I go to the fridge, pull out a Diet Coke, and bring it to her, cracking open the top and pressing the cold can into her hand. "Caffeine, baby," I mutter. "Quinn, bud. Your backpack is there. Donuts are on the counter, and juice and milk are in the fridge if you want something to eat before you brush your teeth."

The drowsiness slides from his expression, excitement filling his eyes. "Did you get sprinkle ones?"

"Quinn!" Belle gasps. "You can't—"

"Are donuts even donuts without sprinkles?" I ask lightly.

Quinn grins and moves to the box, pulling open the lid and snagging two donuts. One is devoured before he turns for the fridge, and I see Belle's cheeks go pink, her mouth opening again, a reproach for the kid likely on her tongue.

"Drink, baby," I order quietly, nudging up the can, distracting her before the rebuke can escape. Then I go to the cabinet and snag a glass, setting it on the counter while Quinn unearths the milk from the fridge. "You good pouring it one-handed?" I ask him, amusement curling through me as he starts in on the second donut.

He nods, speaks through a mouth full of delicious baked good—something I can vouch for considering I had two myself on the drive home, "Thanks, West." Which, of course, sounds like "Smanks, Vest."

Belle sighs, rubbing at her forehead.

But she lifts the can to her lips again and drinks deeply.

Caffeine fix incoming.

I fight a smile as I walk back over to her, murmuring, "Your bag is next to Quinn's, and your car is in the driveway." I drove over and got it this morning then took an Uber back to my car, picked up donuts, more Diet Coke, and now we're here.

The can hits the counter, her eyes come to mine. "You don't

have to do this…" A nod to the donuts, to the front of the house. "Didn't have to do *that*."

"I *wanted* to do it." I shrug. "Bonus is, I got to eat some donuts."

"We'll get out of here as soon as I—"

"Belle." I wait until she looks at me. "Seriously, there's no rush. I've got a big house, and it's empty." I bump her shoulder with mine when she starts to protest again. "Way I see it is that you're doing me a favor by filling the rooms up."

Another sigh.

But I see the relief in her eyes.

So, I cross a line.

Because I know she won't be able to say no if her kid says yes.

"Quinn?" I ask.

He stops, spins to face me, mid third donut consumption. "Yeah?" he says, the word garbled.

Belle groans softly.

"I'm out of town a lot and could use someone to watch the house when I'm gone. You cool if you and your mom stay here for a bit to help me out?"

His eyes go wide and he looks around. "*Here?*"

"I trust your mom," I say turning my gaze to Belle, watching her eyes go wide too. "And I know she raised a good kid. Plus," I add, my lips turning up. "I need someone to play Xbox with when I'm actually here."

None of that is a lie—the empty house, spending far too much time alone when I'm here, the loneliness always creeping in.

Belle's eyes have gone wide.

Quinn runs over to her. "Can we do it, Mom? Can we help West out?"

Her surprise quickly turns to anger.

But not at her son.

Instead, she turns murder-filled eyes my direction, opens her mouth, and—

I dive in to stop the blow-up.

"What time does school start?"

EIGHT

Belle

I SNAG the bag of groceries from the trunk of my car and
freeze.

Because a male arm is reaching by me, brushing my hand
away, grabbing all the handles of the bags at once, and hauling
them out of the trunk.

My body is tense...but not from surprise.

Every time I've shown up with something to carry in from
my car over the last month, West has been there...or well, *here.*

Popping up behind me, snagging whatever I need to bring
inside, not taking no for an answer.

"I'll grab that one," Quinn says, having unbuckled and
rounded the back of the car.

And my son doesn't take no for an answer either with the
tasks that West has inserted himself in—those being carrying
things inside for me, taking the trash out, and...turning the
channels on the remote at warp speed.

Okay, that's not fair.

Or not entirely, anyway.

West is also big on dishes, and cooking dinner, and moving my laundry around when I forget it in the washer, and helping Quinn with his homework, and...

He's a good roommate.

He's a good man.

And...I *still* can't believe the nerve of him, going around me, getting Quinn on his side in a way that meant I couldn't pack us up and go.

Not that I could have done that anyway.

We didn't have anywhere to go, and he gave me an out, and we weren't even late for school.

Because I couldn't say no.

And Quinn didn't want me to.

Neither did West.

And, frankly, he also wasn't wrong about being out of town a lot.

I swear that Quinn and I have spent more time in his house than he has over the last few weeks.

So much time I'm worried that Quinn is getting *too* used to the space, to the luxury, to something I won't ever be able to provide him.

Hell, I'm worried *I'm* getting too attached to it.

The consistently hot water, the space, the quiet. No people pounding around overhead. No neighbors screaming through the walls—or worse. The back yard where Quinn and I can kick a soccer ball around, the driveway with a basketball hoop he can utilize any time and I don't have to worry about him being safe.

West gave us—*me*—that.

And now he's also bringing in my groceries.

Groceries I can afford because he refuses to accept money for rent, money for utilities, money for anything.

Because...we're *watching* his house.

Yeah, I'm thinking that with air quotes.

Because he has a cleaner who comes in weekly, a gardener who does the same, a chef who stocks the fridge for his meal plan meals twice a month.

"I told you," West says quietly as Quinn carries the bag into the house, "that I would go to the store tomorrow."

"You got home at four in the morning," I say, slamming the trunk and hitching my purse higher on my shoulder. "You need food and rest. Plus," I add quietly, "it's the least I can do."

He stops beside me, eyes coming to mine. "Belle," he murmurs.

I shake my head, start walking up the drive. "It's nothing," I begin.

"You're supposed to be getting ahead," he grumbles. "Not feeding me."

I touch his arm. "I'm fine."

"Belle—"

"I'm—*we're*—fine," I snap.

One second, I'm walking through the garage.

The next, the bags of groceries are on the floor and my back is against the wall.

"I—"

His head drops, bringing our mouths so close I can feel his words on my lips. "You don't need to pay me back, baby." His eyes flare with frustration. His body is mere inches away.

And that feels so good that I forget to guard myself.

And the words...they slip free. "You don't understand."

He doesn't move, but his voice is gentle. "What don't I understand?"

"That I have to do *anything* I can to pay you back—"

Another flash of frustration through his eyes. "Belle—"

I press a finger to his lips. "You saved us, saved me. You didn't have to, and you haven't asked anything of me and—"

"You're taking care of my—"

"No, honey," I whisper over the slightly muffled statement. "Don't even try it. I appreciate that you gave me an excuse, saved face with my kid, but let's not look at this as anything else aside from what it is—charity."

He inhales sharply.

"Charity you were not obligated to give me, considering how I came back into your life and how I left it—"

Now it's his turn to press a finger to my lips.

"Bella bee," he murmurs and my heart pulses at the nickname. It's been so long since I've heard it. "You think for a moment I got a second chance at getting to know you, got a glimpse of the woman you are today, the goodness that's the kid you made in there"—he jerks his head to the house—"and think it's *charity?*" A sharp shake of his head. "You've lost your fucking mind."

I exhale and it's shaky.

"I've been in awe of you from the moment I first saw you killing it in dodgeball on the playground in third grade." His lips twitch. "And I fell for you when you punched Billy Conners in the nose for stealing Davie's lunch in fifth."

Surprised laughter slides out of me, and his face goes so soft that my heart squeezes.

Because his words settle deep inside me.

"And the first time I heard you laugh, I knew you'd be in my heart forever." He bends a little, eyes holding mine with piercing intent. "You've always been the woman who haunted my dreams...and now you're *here.*"

My pulse is pounding through my veins, stealing my breath, making my head spin.

"So, baby," he murmurs, stroking a hand lightly up and

down my side. "Just...settle. Stay here in my house, gain a little breathing room, give us time to learn each other again and see what comes of that. Let me get to know that awesome kid you have some more, and just...give us a chance, a *real* chance."

"To see what comes of learning each other again?" I ask, heart in my throat, my voice raspy. "To have a second chance w-with *me?*"

His eyes dance, and he cups my cheek. "I said all of that and you don't think I want another chance with you, Bella bee?"

I don't have any idea how to reply to that.

How to put into words what that gentle, teasing question does to me.

Because I want that so badly—to stay here, to learn him again, to keep him forever.

Because I've wanted it from the moment I broke us to give West a chance at his future.

But I don't have a chance to ponder my reply, to speak it out loud.

Because Quinn's voice echoes from inside the house.

"Mom! West! You coming?"

NINE

West

"GET IT!"

Grunting, practically straining something as I kick out my leg (hello, groin muscles), I manage to get my foot beneath the ball and chip it back over to Quinn.

"Yes!" he shouts, running forward a few steps and catching it on his chest, allowing it to roll down to his feet.

The kid is a *good* soccer player.

His touches are controlled and natural, and he's a fuck of a lot better at kicking the ball around than I am.

Hence the groin straining.

He flicks it back to me and I'm a lot less natural, but I manage to corral it and pass it back—something I accomplish only two more times before Belle pokes her head out into the back yard, face softening when she catches sight of us, and calls, "Dinner will be ready in ten! Time to wash up, honey."

She's talking to Quinn.

But she's also talking to me.

And I can't lie, I fucking love that—the *honey*, the soft expression on her face as she calls that, the similarly soft one she wore when she shooed Quinn outside to "touch grass" and didn't comment when I joined him.

She just smiled.

Same as she had when she came into the house this afternoon with a grocery bag (though Quinn had actually carried it in for her) and grinned at me before I could protest, saying, "Chicken pot pie for dinner tonight!"

My favorite.

Years ago, she was the one who made it for me the first time.

Today I know it means she's trying. She's settling. She's giving us the time I asked for.

And I fucking love that too.

"You play soccer for a team?" I ask as Quinn scoops up the ball and we move to the back door she left propped open.

"Nah," Quinn says. "Soccer's fun, but I think I'd rather learn how to play hockey like you."

I freeze.

And I'm not the only one.

Belle's at the mouth of the hall, and she spins and glances back at me, eyes wide. I can already read what's in her mind— soccer is cheap, just a ball, some shin guards, and cleats. But hockey has a big buy-in—the equipment alone, but also adding the league fees, on-ice training, *off*-ice training, travel...it's a giant hurdle.

But if this kid—this gracious, polite, good-hearted, hard-working kid who's smart and respectful and loves his mom— wants to try hockey, this kid is going to fucking *try hockey*.

"First step of playing hockey is learning how to skate," I tell him.

His face falls. "I've never been."

"Well, the good news is the team is having a family skate next weekend, wanna give it a try?"

His eyes widen. "Really?"

"Yup. It's on Saturday and the whole team will be there."

He's practically vibrating with excitement as he turns to Belle. "Is that okay, Mom? Could I try out skating?"

A blip of quiet, resignation sliding through her features.

But then her face goes soft again and she nods. "Yeah, baby."

He spins back to me. "Then that would be awesome, West. Thank you so much."

See? Polite.

"Are you going to learn to skate too, Mom?"

My lips curve and I answer for her. "Your mom's a great skater—or she was back in high school."

His eyes go wide. "Really?"

I nod.

"Whoa, Mom."

"Upping my cool factor," she says lightly, moving close and ruffling Quinn's hair. "But don't get your hopes up. I'm sure I'm out of practice." She's grinning as she jerks her head toward the bathroom. "Let's wash up first and worry about strapping blades to our feet later, 'kay?"

"Okay!"

He takes off for the bathroom, shutting the door, and I barely have the chance to take a step before she's snagging my arm and dragging me into the kitchen. "Baby—"

She spins to face me. "You don't have to do this."

I exhale, cup her cheeks, practically willing her to understand this once and for all. "Why don't you understand that I *know* that, baby? That all I've offered, all I'm *continuing* to offer is because I like you, I like Quinn, and I *want* to do it."

"You shouldn't," she whispers.

"Share the wealth?" I ask sweeping a hand around the space. "If you haven't seen, I have plenty, so having you guys here isn't a hit on my bank account. And I like that my house isn't empty when I'm gone, that you guys are here when I am. As far as I figure, you're the reason I have all this, so you get to share in it."

"That makes no sense."

"If you hadn't broken up with me," I remind her. "I wouldn't have kept going, baby. I would have eventually come home, lived a small life, given up on my dreams. *You* gave me the freedom to go and the drive to keep playing."

"No, I *hurt* you."

I stroke my thumb over her cheek. "I don't care."

"West—"

"I *don't* care." I settle my forehead against hers. "You and Quinn are both here now and you need to shut up and deal because you're stuck with me."

She sighs. "I hate that it feels the other way around."

"No comments on me telling you to shut up?"

Her eyes close for a minute before opening again. "West," she murmurs, "you're being deliberately obtuse."

I touch my mouth to hers. "Are you not cooking me my favorite meal?" I ask against her lips. "My stomach won't ever let you go."

She laughs.

I'm glad because I know that my heart won't let her go either. But I keep that thought in my head. Because all of this has already been hard enough for her to accept.

"Better, baby," I say softly. "Just stay the course, give us this time, keep moving forward."

She exhales. "You make this all sound so easy."

"Isn't it?"

Her brows drag together.

"Hasn't it been easy?" I press. "Hasn't it *felt* easy and natural and exactly the same as before?" Minus the sex and cuddling and kissing.

Well, maybe not minus the last.

Because her expression is so befuddled that I can't resist bending, pressing my mouth to hers again, longer this time.

And *that's* exactly like before.

And also so much better.

She immediately melts against me, her body coming flush to mine, her lips parting, her tongue stroking across mine—

"Why are you kissing my mom?"

We both still.

Then Belle tears her mouth from mine. It's swollen and reddened and slick—beyond tempting.

But I table my need and turn to face Quinn.

"I like your mom," I tell him. "When grownups like each other sometimes they kiss."

"Well, yeah." He shrugs. "But does this mean you guys are boyfriend and girlfriend yet?"

Yet.

God, the kid is smart.

"I'd like that," I tell him. "But I'm still working on convincing your mom to want me as her boyfriend."

Belle gasps, nails pressing into my chest.

I smother my smother, ignore her angry eyes. "If she agrees, I'll let you know, okay?"

His gaze goes from mine to his mom, whose cheeks flush bright pink.

Then he shrugs again.

"'Kay." A beat. "Is dinner ready?"

IT COMES as no surprise that Quinn's natural athleticism carries over onto the ice.

After a few shaky laps, he found his stride and is currently flying around the rink with a group of Eagles kids, all acting like tiny maniacs.

Grinning, I step off the rink and make my way to Belle.

She's sipping hot chocolate from a paper cup, her nose adorably pink from the cold.

"Thank you for this," she whispers as I sit next to her and swipe the cup, stealing a sip.

"Baby?" I ask.

Her eyes are on Quinn as I press the cup back into her hand, but I wait for them to drift to mine. "Yeah?" she murmurs when she's finally gazing at me again and I don't immediately speak.

I touch her cheek. "Stop saying thank you for everything."

Warmth in those eyes. Then she exhales softly and leans against my shoulder, the contact sending a bolt of heat through me. I've snuck a few kisses over the last week, but not nearly enough to soothe the constant need churning through my insides.

Even having her this close makes my nerves stand on edge, my fingers tingle with the need to touch her, my cock twitch and threaten to get hard.

I shove that down.

Mostly because she's talking. "I'm here."

I frown. Talking but making no sense.

She settles her free hand on my thigh, something that does nothing to soothe that raw, aching need shooting through me.

"Do you get it?"

I shake my head.

"I'm here. Quinn is out there. I'm not going to stop saying thank you—"

I open my mouth, but she cuts me off.

"But I'm also not going anywhere."

She leans in, brushes her lips across my jaw. "Because I'm giving us time."

My heart skips a beat, hope surging through me.

God, I love this woman. I don't think I ever stopped, even for that brief period of time when I hated her, I still loved her.

"Bella bee," I murmur.

Her mouth curves. "I've always loved it when you called me that."

"I know." I tilt her head up, leaning closer, my mouth brushing ever so lightly over hers. Then again.

And again.

And—

"Mom!" Quinn shouts. "Stop kissing West and get out here!"

Everyone on the ice seems to freeze, and I don't miss that my teammates King, Rome, and Cam—all recently matched up with women of their own—look at each other and grin.

Same as I don't miss that Hudson, one of the newer guys on the team, same as me, looks at his skates, a muscle jumping in his thigh.

He's been a surly fuck of late, especially since the team hired a new head coach.

But I don't have time to focus on my grumpy teammate—or the way his eyes linger on Diana, said head coach who's crouched near the bench, head tossed back as she laughs at something a little kid says.

I don't have time because Belle is tossing the empty hot cocoa cup into the trash and jumping to her feet, her free hand wrapping around mine.

"Less kissing," she teases. "More skating."

TEN

Belle

"BELLE?"

I freeze—mid tuck of my purse over my shoulder—at the sound of my boss, Jace Henderson's, voice. "Yes?"

"Can you come in here a second?"

My throat gets tight.

Because that question...it sounds angry.

Have I fucked something up?

What if Jace doesn't want me here any longer? What if he's found someone better? Someone more qualified? Someone with a college degree and years and years of experience?

Panic slices through my middle.

Quinn. Oh God, how will I take care of Quinn?

But just as quickly as that panic comes on, it dissipates. Because I remember...I'm not alone.

I'm *not* alone.

Whatever is coming, I don't have to face it alone.

Holding those words tight, I lift my chin, shore up my spine, and walk into Jace's office. He owns a conglomeration of media companies in the Bay Area—and abroad—and is a very powerful man.

One who took a chance on me.

One who gave me time off when Quinn was sick.

One who—

"Belle?"

I jump, stop staying stuck in my head, and focus on Jace.

He's holding a sheaf of papers...and yup, he's pissed.

"What the fuck is this?" he snaps, tossing them on the desk.

Hesitantly, I shuffle closer, eyes going to the papers...and then shooting up to connect with his.

"You didn't tell me the insurance company was fucking you and Quinn over," he growls, tossing another stack onto the desktop. "And you didn't tell me that you two were fucking *homeless.*"

"I—"

"What the fuck, Belle?" he snaps. "You're my assistant, yes, but you're a whole lot more. You're a person I care about, and you got *evicted* because you couldn't pay bills for your son's hospital stay. Why didn't you come to me? Why didn't you *tell* me?"

"I—"

"I'm a goddamned billionaire!" He slams his fist next to the papers, sending them fluttering through the air. "Did you ever think that maybe I could help?"

"I—"

He drops his palms to the desk, pushes up to his feet, voice calming, though it's still liberally laced with ice. "Did you ever stop to think I would *want* to help? I care about you and Quinn."

"I—" I begin again. Then pause, half expecting him to interrupt me for the umpteenth time. When he doesn't, I say, "It wasn't your problem."

Which is the *wrong* thing to say.

His scowl deepens to insane proportions. "Not my problem," he grits out, shoving a hand through his hair, mussing the locks in a sure sign that he's about to lose it. "Not *my* problem?"

"I—" I bite back my excuses and sigh. "Look," I say carefully. "I didn't think it was anyone's problem but mine. And I was too stubborn to recognize that I didn't have to do it all on my own." An exhale. "But I've learned—or *am* learning that I don't need to do it that way, that I have people who'll take my back, and"—I reach over and squeeze his arm—"I'm also lucky enough to have a boss who cares about me."

The anger bleeds out of his face. "You do," he says gently before his eyes fill with warning. "And you also have a boss who won't take no when it comes to giving you this."

He passes me an envelope and when I open the top, pull out the papers, my heart convulses.

"Jace," I murmur.

"Don't argue with me today," he grumbles. "And don't say no. Just...consider it and know that you'll have to come up with a damned good argument to get me to back off about it."

I open my mouth, but he just snags his jacket and phone, glares at me and semi-repeats, "A *damned* good one."

And then he's sweeping from the room in a cloud of grumpy, billionaire yumminess.

I stare after him from a couple of seconds then shake my head and know that, as dire as things were, what I told Jace is correct.

I'm not alone.

I just didn't understand that was *always* the case.

But the medical bills—now paid—and the apartment in Quinn's school district funded by Jace's company is proof of that.

Just as much as West opening his house and kissing me gently and teaching Quinn how to skate is even more so.

We're not alone.

Smiling, I shove the papers into my purse and hurry out of the office.

I have a sleepover to drop Quinn off at.

And...I have a man to get home to.

I'M THINKING of all the things I want to tell West the entire drive to Quinn's sleepover.

How I'm finally understanding, finally accepting, finally open to more from my future. How I want him to know that *I* want to know what a good relationship can be like, to know how it feels to not have to struggle and do it all alone.

And that's thanks to him.

So, I spend the drive back to the house pondering and planning and rehearsing my speech, wanting West to know exactly how much all of this has meant to me.

But then I walk into the kitchen.

And I smell what he's cooking.

And that plan slips right out of my head.

Because tonight he's cooking *my* favorite meal.

And he's turning and smiling at me, putting the spoon he's using to stir the potato and leek soup down onto a folded paper towel then moving across the room. "Hey, Bella bee," he murmurs, reaching for me, brushing his lips over my forehead before slipping his fingers beneath the strap of my purse and tugging it down my arm.

Or part of the way, anyway.

Because it's barely reached my elbow when all the love in my belly explodes outward—not in words, but in action.

I launch myself into his arms, lift my mouth to his...

And kiss him with everything I'm feeling so brightly in my heart.

ELEVEN

West

I ONLY GET a glimpse of her face—and the flash of the heat and need and affection in her eyes has every cell in my body freezing.

But then *her* body is colliding with mine and I'm not seeing, not thinking, not trying to discern what all of that emotion means.

I'm *feeling*.

Her lush tits against my chest.

Her arms wrapping around me.

Her hands sliding up my back, diving into my hair.

Her lips hitting mine.

I groan, slip my arm around her waist and haul her against me, deepening the kiss—this first kiss she's initiated since she's been back in my life. Soft lips and lush tits. A moan vibrating along my tongue. Hips undulating against mine.

I kiss her with all the need that's built up over the last decade, all the lonely nights, the empty beds, the missed moments, the *struggle*, and—no surprise—it quickly gets out of hand.

"Bedroom," she rasps, tearing her lips from mine, her chest heaving.

Swollen lips. Pink cheeks. Needy eyes.

Yeah, definitely time for the bedroom.

I don't delay, just bend slightly and scoop her up, cradling her against my chest as I hit the hall, climb the stairs, and move into my bedroom.

Settling her onto my mattress is a fucking dream, a fucking fantasy.

"Come here," she whispers when I hesitate at the side of the bed.

"You sure?" I whisper back.

"West?"

I touch her cheek. "Yeah, baby?"

"I like you too," she murmurs, referencing our conversation from the other day as she reaches for me, drawing me down over her. "So much. And I like what we're doing and...I want more."

My heart rolls over in my chest.

"I want you."

"Baby." It's gravel. It's barely discernible.

"I want *everything*."

"*Belle*."

I know she gets it—how much that means to me, how much I want that, want her—because she smiles, lifts up onto her elbows and says, "All of which means that now you get to show me all the things you've learned over the last decade."

I grin.

Then I take her up on that challenge.

I kiss her again, but this time I pair it with slipping my hand beneath her blouse, trailing it along soft skin, drawing it up. I pair it with dragging my mouth down her throat, undoing the buttons of her shirt, parting the material, exposing her to me.

"God, you're beautiful," I groan.

Her mouth hitches up as I kiss my way toward her breasts. "I'm not sixteen anymore."

I flick open the front clasp of her bra, bury my face in her tits. "You also didn't have *these* a decade ago."

Her breath catches and I don't waste any more time talking.

I kiss my way over to one taut nipple, suck deeply, rolling the sensitive bud on my tongue, massage the lush tit that's driven me crazy over the last two months. I listen to her moans, her shuddering breaths, the sexy movements of her hips and body to learn what she likes today.

It's things she liked in the past—

And it's more.

My teeth on her skin, my fingers trailing over her flesh then flicking open the button on her slacks, dipping beneath the waistband, beneath her underwear, sliding into slick folds.

"Wet," I growl, moving down her body, dragging off her pants, her underwear. "*Mine.*"

Then I toss her legs over my shoulders and I get down to showing her all the skills I've acquired over the years. I fuck her with my tongue, with my fingers, suck and lick her clit. I find all the spots that make her moan and I slowly drive her up...

And then over the edge.

"West!" she cries out, her legs clenching around me, her hips bucking, her pussy clamping around my fingers.

Fuck, she's beautiful.

Fuck, I want to taste her again.

But my dick is about to break in half.

So, this time I'm not slow or gentle as I wind her pleasure tighter and tighter, as I bring her closer and closer to the edge.

She grinds her pussy against my mouth, her tits bouncing, her lungs working, her moans slowly driving me insane.

Only when she's a hairsbreadth away from exploding do I reach for the nightstand, pull out a condom.

I'm rolling it down my dick a heartbeat later.

And then I'm kneeling between her legs, notching myself at her entrance, desperate to thrust deep. But I force myself to stop, to wait for her eyes to come to mine. "Still good, baby?"

Her cheeks are pink.

Her eyes are warm.

Her words are exactly what I'm desperate to hear.

"Come inside me, honey."

I don't hesitate. I thrust deep—and fuck, it's perfection. It's *too* fucking good, so good that I'm ready to explode on that first stroke.

Thankfully, she's right there with me, meeting me thrust for thrust, nails biting into my skin, pussy convulsing around my cock. It would be embarrassingly fast if she wasn't coming too, if she wasn't calling out my name and falling apart.

But she is.

And so am I—my orgasm blasting through me, sending my strokes into jerky disarray as pleasure tears through my insides, sucking the strength through my limbs, sending me collapsing on top of her.

I barely have the presence of mind to roll to the side.

But I do, and I spend the next minutes trying to catch my breath and summon the strength to speak.

Only, before I can, her stomach rumbles.

"Shit," she mutters. "I skipped lunch."

Suddenly, I'm not tired. I have to feed my woman. Drawing her closer, I nuzzle at her throat. "Stay here, Bella bee. I'll go grab us some food from the kitchen."

Her face is soft, and she touches my cheek. "Thank you, honey."

A nip to her throat. "It's selfish, really." I grin. "This way I get to keep you naked."

She giggles, and I shove out of bed, snagging my jeans and tugging them on.

Then I'm making my way into the kitchen, thanking my lucky stars that the soup is on simmer and my hard work isn't ruined after the side trip to the bedroom.

And what a side trip it was.

Grin widening, I bend and scoop up her purse, shaking my head at the mess I made—keys and gum scattered, wallet half out, lipstick rolled beneath the toe kick of the cabinets, papers scattered.

I gather all her shit, stuff it inside, but when I make it to the papers...

I frown.

Because, although it takes me a second, I eventually realize the document in my hands is the paperwork for...

A lease on an apartment.

TWELVE

Belle

WHEN HE DOESN'T COME BACK UP in a few minutes,
I start to worry.

Then my stomach rumbles again and, his order to remain
naked and wait for him or not, I crawl out of bed, snag his tee,
my underwear (both of which are scattered on opposite sides of
the room, along with the rest of our clothes), and pull them on.

Then I head down the stairs.

Maybe dinner burned. Or he needs a hand carrying everything up.

But when I walk into the kitchen, I find it's empty.

"West?" I call, noting my purse on the counter and the pot
of soup on the stove and...

No sign of my hockey-playing boyfriend.

Maybe he's in the pantry?

But he's not.

Or the bathroom?

Nope. Not there.

How about the laundry room? Likely, I left some laundry in the washer that needs to be moved into the dryer.

Only, he's not in there either.

"West?" I call as I wander back into the kitchen.

There's no answer.

And the soup's simmering on the stove, a bottle of wine and two glasses on the counter next to it...and next to *those*—

My throat threatens to close up.

The lease and information about the apartment Jace gave me this afternoon.

Something West has no explanation for—except for, possibly, the worst sort of one.

Because I jumped him the moment I walked in, and I slept with him—sleeping that didn't actually involve sleeping because it was pure fucking. And I didn't give him the words I was practicing on the way home, the words he needs to hear to know that I have no intention of leaving him again.

And...I didn't tell him I love him.

I just fucked him and he found—

"Shit," I whisper, dread slicing through me.

Dread that whips hard and fast when I hear the garage door start rumbling down.

Oh, God.

He's leaving.

I didn't tell West I love him and he found those papers and now he's *leaving*.

I dash for the hall, sprint toward the garage door, and am just reaching for the handle when it turns beneath my fingers, starts to swing inward.

West freezes in the slender opening, his brows dragging together. "Bella bee? What the hell's the matter?"

"I—" But my words stifle up in my throat because he's standing there. No, he's slipping a hand through the gap in the door, nudging me back, and stepping inside. A heartbeat later, I'm in his arms, one of his hands on my cheek.

"Is Quinn okay?"

The question doesn't make sense with the whirlwind of thoughts in my head. "I—" I shake myself. "Yes," I say. "He was stoked for the sleepover, and I haven't heard anything different." All of a sudden, my heart convulses. Maybe that's why West was taking a long time to come back up. Had something happened? "Did he call you?"

West's fingers tighten slightly, confusion rippling across his face. "No, baby."

"Oh," I whisper.

"So," he says, cupping my jaw, "if the kid's good, want to tell me why you looked so panicked a few seconds ago?"

I open my mouth, but that whirlwind of thoughts takes over again and my throat closes up, my words stuck inside my head.

You love him.

That voice comes loudest of all, quieting down the others.

And it lets *my* voice come.

"I love you!" I blurt.

His fingers flex again and his eyes go wide, and then he opens his mouth.

But now that my words have come, they don't stop.

"And I know you saw the papers," I say, "but I didn't intend to leave without talking to you—or leave at all, really. Even if you want Quinn and I to get our own place, which is totally fine, of course—"

"Baby—"

"But if you want us to stay, I want to stay and I know Quinn does too, even though it's fast and a little bit crazy. But I love you and I love what we're building and I wasn't going to just disappear or force you away from us, I swear I wasn't—"

"Bella bee—"

"My boss was pissed when he found out I hadn't told him I was struggling and he all but shoved the papers into my hands, after paying the rest of Quinn's medical bills. But I swear I wasn't going to do anything without talking to you and Quinn both. And that's not even touching the fact that my boss paid off my bills or that he's grumpy and taciturn and...apparently, a teddy bear who cares about me *and* Quinn. And—"

West slides his thumb over, presses it lightly to my blathering lips, stopping the flood of words.

"I knew you weren't just going to go without a word, baby."

I blink. "How?" I ask against that finger, the question slightly smothered.

"Because I know *you*." His mouth kicks up. "And also because I wasn't going to let you go."

All the air in my lungs rushes out, something that's made easier because his thumb is moving again, trailing lightly over my cheek.

"You weren't?"

Now his mouth flattens out, his eyes holding mine, the fierceness in his gaze stealing my breath again. "No, baby. Because I love you too. Because I've known what my life is like without you, and now that I've gotten you back—gotten the bonus of having Quinn in my life for a short time—there's no fucking way I'm letting either of you go."

"You love me?"

He chuckles softly. "Truthfully, I don't think I ever stopped."

I inhale sharply, and he rests his forehead against mine.

"I get if you need time to be on your own," he says. "But do it while I'm on the road, do it while we're building our new us, and if you absolutely need to live on your own—"

"I don't," I blurt, cupping the side of his neck, keeping him close. "I've spent long enough alone," I tell him. "I'm ready to be here with you."

God, his eyes.

They're so fucking beautiful.

But I only get them for a moment because then he's scooping me up into his arms, marching through the kitchen, and heading straight for the stairs.

"What about eating dinner?" I tease.

He pauses, slants his mouth over mine, kissing me until my lungs protest and teasing is the last thing on my mind. Then he lifts his head. "I'm eating you first."

Heat twining through my insides. "Oh," I whisper. "Okay, then."

He grins and then we're moving up the stairs again.

We're hitting his bedroom, landing on the bed...

And coming together in the most beautiful way possible.

Which is why it's much, *much* later, over bowls of soup, that I remember to ask, "If you weren't leaving after finding the papers, why were you outside?"

He tugs a lock of my hair, smiles.

"You left the garage door open."

I freeze then start laughing.

A new life. A bright future.

And one that's a hell of a lot closer...

All because I left a door open.

THIRTEEN

QUINN'S out on the ice, and it's no surprise to me that he's a natural, flying around, stealing pucks, making shots.

It's a fucking blast to watch him learn, to watch him fall in love with the game.

"He's good," Belle murmurs, eyes trained on the rink.

"Damned good," I agree as he sprints for the bench, completing the change exactly as he should—working hard, getting off to let the next line have their go. I draw her a little closer, tease, "When are we going to get you out there?"

She stills then rolls her eyes as she glances up at me. "I like all of my bones unbroken, thank you very much." Then she leans a little closer, presses her lips to my jaw. "How do you like these early mornings at the rink?"

It's barely eight, and we've been here an hour already.

Youth hockey is brutal.

Still, I'm living a dream, a fantasy. So, I just grin. "Reminds me of my childhood."

"I know," she says, burrowing into my side. "Especially, the freezing my butt off while watching part."

My grin widens and I pull off my coat, wrapping it around her, and then drawing her close before she can argue about accepting it. "Quinn's back out there," I say, nodding at the ice, taking full advantage of her Mom Distraction to keep her warm.

"I wasn't angling for your jacket," she says a minute later, proving that my woman is not to be distracted—or not for long, anyway.

"I know." I kiss the top of her head. "But this has the side benefit of keeping you close."

She sighs, but doesn't protest further, and we watch the rest of Quinn's game all but glued together.

When he comes out of the locker room long minutes later, half carrying, half dragging the bag that weighs almost as much as him, it's to ask, "Can I go to Jake's for a sleepover?"

I love sleepovers.

I especially love that tomorrow is a holiday so that Quinn doesn't have school.

What I don't love is *reciprocating* said sleepovers.

But I take the good with the bad.

"I think you need a shower first, kid," Belle says wisely, "but if Jake's parents say it's okay, I'm good with it. I'll go check with Jodi now."

Quinn glances at me. "We were going to play games tonight, can we do that tomorrow instead?"

Smart kid. Sweet kid.

I reach out and muss his sweaty hair. "Works for me."

"Jodi's down for torture," Belle says, rejoining us a few minutes later. "Though, we're on for next weekend."

I stifle my groan, but know she hears it anyway because her lips curve up.

The next hour is filled with driving home, getting Quinn showered and packed up, and then me dropping him off.

But it's an hour that's punctuated with great.

Because Belle greets me completely naked in the kitchen when I get home.

And I get to fuck her someplace I haven't had the chance to fuck her yet—the kitchen table.

It's great—of course it is—and when it's time to get comfortable and chill, I carry her to the couch, cuddling her close as we watch an action flick on TV.

Between the explosions and car chases, the question that's been eating at me for months now slips out. "Why'd you ask that in the locker room, baby?"

She stills.

Then reaches forward and flicks off the TV.

Her eyes are remorseful. "Why'd I ask you if you're still a player who gives up on the play?"

Yeah. *That.*

It pissed me off, hurt like a bitch—even though I didn't want to admit it at the time.

Because some part of me worried it was true.

I gave up on fighting for her.

"I'm sorry," she whispers. "I know it was out of line."

The guilt's heavy in her eyes, her voice, her frame.

Damn. I shouldn't have brought this shit up, not after all this time.

"Forget it," I say. "It doesn't matter."

"It does, honey."

"I mean it." I brush my lips over hers. "That question brought us back together, baby."

"It hurt you, and pissed you off, and I hate that I asked it. I gave up on us. You—"

Shit. I can see her spiraling now.

I should have just let this go.

"As far as I'm concerned," I say, "it was a line that needed to be crossed. Yeah, it made me mad," I add over her protest. "But without it, we'd still be apart. Now I get you and Quinn, and a life that's not lonely."

Her face softens, and she reaches up, touches my cheek. "I still shouldn't have asked it."

I draw her closer, run my hand up and down her back, and open my mouth.

But I don't get out any further reassurances.

Because her next words steal them away.

"But I made myself do it because I had to know that you were still you."

Everything in me stills.

Then...I get it.

And I love her even more for it.

"You being mad about it," she says hurriedly, "furious and hurt and upset...I knew that the West I knew ten years ago was still in there. I knew that I could trust you and—"

"Shut up."

She blinks, a thread of hurt weaving into her eyes. "*Excuse* me?"

"You can't be sweet," I mock grumble, tugging her on top of me, "and not expect me to react."

Her brow furrows.

"You can't be sweet and not expect me to kiss you."

The lines smooth out.

Then she smiles.

"Well then"—she trails a hand down my chest—"why don't you get on that?"

"I love you," I murmur, brushing my lips over hers. "I love you more for asking that, for understanding my reaction." I give her a long, drugging kiss. "But I love you most of all for giving me you."

"I—"

I take her mouth.

And then I take *her*.

And I do it knowing that neither of us are ever going to let go.

Not ever again.

HUDSON

I'M FUCKED, I realize as I stare up at the tiny spitfire of a woman.

Who's lecturing me.

In a lilting voice that I can't help but get lost in the melody of.

"...and I really need you to take some time to focus on this new system," she saying, gesturing at an iPad. "I know it's new and it's tough to make these changes, but this will make it much easier for us to mobilize your speed and strength."

She pauses.

And I realize that I'm staring.

That I'm so caught up in the beauty of her, I haven't processed she's expecting an answer.

"Got it," I manage to rasp out.

She nods then rounds the desk and moves to the door of her office, pulling it open so I can see the hallway beyond.

Her office.

The new head coach of the Eagles, Diana Connors.

The first female head coach in the league.

And the object of my fantasies since she first showed up at training camp.

"I'll see you out on the ice," she says in that quiet, sure, *melodic* voice.

And...

I'm staring again.

Committing every freckle, every eyelash to memory.

Obsessed.

She clears her throat, brow furrowing. "Hudson?" she asks quietly. "Is everything okay?"

I nod. "Sorry," I mutter, shoving to my feet, and moving to the door, feeling like a fucking lumbering giant as I get close to her. "Just tired," I add by way of explanation. "I'll be good by practice though."

Her expression smooths. "Okay, Huddy," she says. "I'll let you get dressed."

That does something to me.

No, not *something*.

Her soft voice calling me my nickname wraps invisible fingers around my cock and strokes.

Stupid.

I bob my head at her and start to step into the hall.

"Huddy?"

I stop, glance over my shoulder.

She opens her mouth.

But I never do hear her question...

Because that moment, the world starts violently shaking.

THANK YOU FOR READING! I hope you loved Belle and West second chance love story as much as I enjoyed writing it! The next full-length book in the Eagles Hockey series is LUCKY

LACES. **I thought I had my whole life figured out…
and then the world started shaking.**

CLICK HERE TO READ LUCKY LACES NOW>

AND ARE you curious about Jace Henderson, grumpy boss with a heart of gold? Check out a sneak peek of his happy ending below in BEAUTY & THE BOARDROOM. **She's completely wrong for me…but I can't stay away.**

CLICK HERE TO READ BEAUTY & THE BOARD-ROOM NOW>

Marie

I reach for the handle of the sedan that's just pulled to a stop at the curb—

Only to find my fingers brushed away.

Starting, my head jerks up, focus yanked from my phone, and I glare at the man who's similarly focused on his phone and, apparently, not noticing that this is *my* freaking car.

"What the hell are you doing?" I snap, brushing *his* fingers away.

He glances up, as though shocked that other people exist on Earth with him.

And given the brand of that suit—something I know because my boss, Jean-Michel Dubois, wears the same expensive designer—this man doesn't likely interact with the common people.

"What *are* you doing?" he snaps back.

"This is my Lyft."

I yank at the door, start to step into the opening.

But before I get there, his hand is on my arm, stopping me.

"Don't touch me," I growl.

He steps back, breaking contact and lifting his hands, palms out in surrender. "Fuck, woman." A scowl that does nothing to dampen the model-esque beauty of his features.

Gorgeous face.

Sexy body that *fills out* that expensive suit—broad shoulders, flat stomach, thick thighs.

Too bad he's an asshole.

Something he proves by what he says next.

"I don't know what mental hospital you've just checked yourself out of, but I have a meeting I need to get to"—he nods at the car—"in *my* Lyft, and I don't have time to fuck around."

I glance at my phone screen then back up at the car.

The make and model match.

My app tells me my ride is here.

And this asshole is trying to take my car?

What's he even going to do when it takes him to the wrong place?

Part of me is tempted to step back and let him find out.

The rest of me is outraged.

Because I have far too much experience with men being assholes and trying to take advantage of me.

"I don't have time to 'fuck around'"—I make air quotes—"either. I have important things to do this evening too."

It's a lie.

For once, I'm not working tonight.

My plans are to soak until I'm turned into a wrinkle puddle of woman in my bathtub, drink an entire bottle of Oak Ridge wine, and then pass out with a cooking show on in the background.

But this man doesn't know that.

And, frankly, his meeting isn't more important than my life.

I lift my phone, pointing the screen in his direction. "This is *my* ride. See?"

His expression hardens, but only for a moment before he leans in and seems to stare at my phone. He straightens and something strange crawls across his hazel eyes.

It almost looks like amusement.

But that can't be right because he steps back, waves a hand toward the open door, and says, "My mistake."

I scowl at him.

That's right.

It's *his* mistake.

Chin lifting, huff escaping, I dump my bag onto the seat and slide in, reaching for the door—

Only to find my fingers brushed away again.

The man pokes his gorgeous head in, one dark lock of hair falling over his face, calling for female fingers to push it back. "I'll get that for you."

Before I can reply, he's shutting it, stepping back.

Men.

Ugh.

I sigh and start to settle back on the leather seat.

Only I freeze, horror slicing my insides to ribbons.

Because I hear,

"Jace Henderson?"

And I realize that this isn't my car after all.

CLICK HERE TO READ BEAUTY & THE BOARDROOM NOW>

Hate missing Elise's new releases? Love contests, exclusive excerpts and giveaways?
Then signup for Elise's newsletter here!

www.elisefaber.com/newsletter

And join Elise's fan group, the Fabinators (https://www.facebook.com/groups/fabinators) for insider information, sneak peaks at new releases, and fun freebies! Hope to see you there!

If you enjoy my series, considering supporting me on PATREON! Get access to early releases, bonus content, character art, audiobooks, special edition covers, swag, and much more!

CLICK HERE TO SUPPORT ME>

I so appreciate your help in spreading the word about my books, including sharing with friends! Please leave a review on your favorite book site!

EAGLES HOCKEY SERIES

Eagles Hockey Series (all stand alone)
Broken Laces
Lace 'em Up
Knotted Laces
Loaded Laces
Lucky Laces

ALSO BY ELISE FABER

***Gold Hockey* (all stand alone)**

Blocked

Backhand

Boarding

Benched

Breakaway

Breakout

Checked

Coasting

Centered

Charging

Caged

Crashed

A Gold Christmas

Cycled

Caught

Cap

Covered

Crushed

Changed

Scored

***Breakers Hockey* (all stand alone)**

Broken

Boldly

Breathless

Ballsy

Bewitched

Blowout

Breathe

Blazed

Sierra Hockey Series

Over the Line

Caught from Behind

The Big Skate

On the Fly

Eagles Hockey Series (all stand alone)

Broken Laces

Lace 'em Up

Knotted Laces

Loaded Laces

Lucky Laces

Oak Ridge Vineyards

Bottles & Blades

Beauty & the Boardroom

Rush Hockey Trilogy #1

Big Puck Energy

Filthy Puckboy

So Pucking Over It

Rush Hockey Trilogy #2

Love, Pucks, and Other Stories

All's Fair in Pucks and War

No Pucks Lost Between Us

Rush Hockey Novellas

Puck and Make Up

Billionaire's Club (all stand alone)

Bad Night Stand

Bad Breakup

Bad Husband

Bad Hookup

Bad Divorce

Bad Fiancé

Bad Boyfriend

Bad Blind Date

Bad Wedding

Bad Engagement

Bad Bridesmaid

Bad Swipe

Bad Girlfriend

Bad Best Friend

Bad Rebound

Bad Romance

Bad Business

Bad Billionaire's Quickies

***Love, Action, Camera* (all stand alone)**

Dotted Line

Action Shot

Close-Up

End Scene

Meet Cute

***Love After Midnight* (all stand alone)**

Rum And Notes

Virgin Daiquiri

On The Rocks

Sex On The Seats

Life Sucks Series

Train Wreck

Hot Mess

Dumpster Fire

Clusterf*@k

FUBAR

Perfect Storm

Free Fall

Lost Cause

***Roosevelt Ranch Series* (all stand alone, series complete)**

Disaster at Roosevelt Ranch

Heartbreak at Roosevelt Ranch

Collision at Roosevelt Ranch

Regret at Roosevelt Ranch

Desire at Roosevelt Ranch

***Phoenix Series* (read in order)**

Phoenix Rising

Dark Phoenix

Phoenix Freed

***Phoenix: LexTal Chronicles* (rereleasing soon, stand alone, Phoenix world)**

From Ashes

In Flames

To Smoke

***KTS Series* (all stand alone, series complete)**

Riding The Edge

Crossing The Line

Leveling The Field

Scorching The Earth

Cocky Heroes World

Tattooed Troublemaker

ABOUT THE AUTHOR

USA Today bestselling author, Elise Faber, loves chocolate, Star Wars, Harry Potter, and hockey (the order depending on the day and how well her team -- the Sharks! -- are playing). She and her husband also play as much hockey as they can squeeze into their schedules, so much so that their typical date night is spent on the ice. Elise is the mom to two exuberant boys and lives in Northern California. Connect with her in her Facebook group, the Fabinators or find more information about her books at www.elisefaber.com.

facebook.com/elisefaberauthor

amazon.com/author/elisefaber

bookbub.com/profile/elise-faber

instagram.com/elisefaber

tiktok.com/@elisefaberauthor

goodreads.com/elisefaber